KT-363-073

For Sabrina B. and Zoë Z.

First published in Great Britain in 1995 by Andersen Press Ltd.,
20 Vauxhall Bridge Road, London SW1V 2SA.
This paperback edition first published in 2010 by Andersen Press Ltd.
Copyright © David McKee, 1995
The rights of David McKee to be identified as the author and illustrator
of this work have been asserted by him in accordance with
the Copyright, Designs and Patents Act, 1988.
All rights reserved.
Colour separated in Switzerland by Photolitho AG, Zürich.
Printed and bound in China.

10   9   8   7   6   5   4   3   2

British Library Cataloguing in Publication Data available.

ISBN 978 1 84939 135 1

ELMER
in the Snow

David McKee

Andersen Press

One morning, Elmer, the patchwork elephant, met a group of elephants who didn't look very happy.

"What's the matter?" asked Elmer.

"What's the matter is that it's cold," said one of the elephants. "That's what's the matter."

"It's not really cold," said Elmer. "It's just a bit colder than usual. What you need is a good walk to warm you up. Come on, come with me."

Elmer led the elephants in a direction they
didn't normally go. The way went steeply
upwards and the elephants were soon puffing
with the effort.

"I'm very warm now, thank you Elmer," said
one of the elephants. "Shall we go back now?"

"Not yet," said Elmer. "Keep going."

After they had gone further, an elephant said,
"Elmer, look at the trees, they're different here."
"That's because we are so high up," said Elmer.
"Come on, there's something I want to show you."

A little later the elephants came out into the open and they stared at the sight – everywhere was white. "SNOW!" they shouted. Although they had heard about snow, this was the first time they had actually seen any. The elephants rushed forward and roared with laughter as they played in the snow.

"It's really cold," called one of the elephants.

"Cold but fun," laughed another.

"Now, come and look at this," called Elmer.
He was sliding on the ice of a pond that had
frozen solid. One by one the others curiously
joined him.

Soon the elephants were slipping and sliding and crashing and falling and really enjoying themselves. They didn't notice Elmer quietly sneak away.

The elephants forgot all about Elmer until they heard his voice nearby.
"Help! Help! I've frozen solid."
The elephants stopped playing and hurried to find Elmer. To their dismay, there stood a white elephant.
"He has, he's frozen solid," gasped one of the elephants.

Then he touched the white elephant and a
piece fell off. "It's made of snow," he said.
"I know where Elmer is," chuckled another. He pointed
to a line of footprints in the snow.
"Come on."

The elephants followed the line of footprints but before they reached him, Elmer appeared and with a laugh, started throwing snowballs that he had already prepared.

It wasn't long before all the elephants were throwing snowballs at each other.

"It's starting to snow quite hard," said Elmer
after a while. "It's time for us to go."
Still laughing and playing, and with the snow
falling all around them, the elephants hurried
back to the trees and then on home.

When they were finally home again,
one of the elephants said, "Snow is fun,
but it really is cold."
"Yes," said another. "It's nice to be back in the warm."
Elmer said nothing. He just smiled.

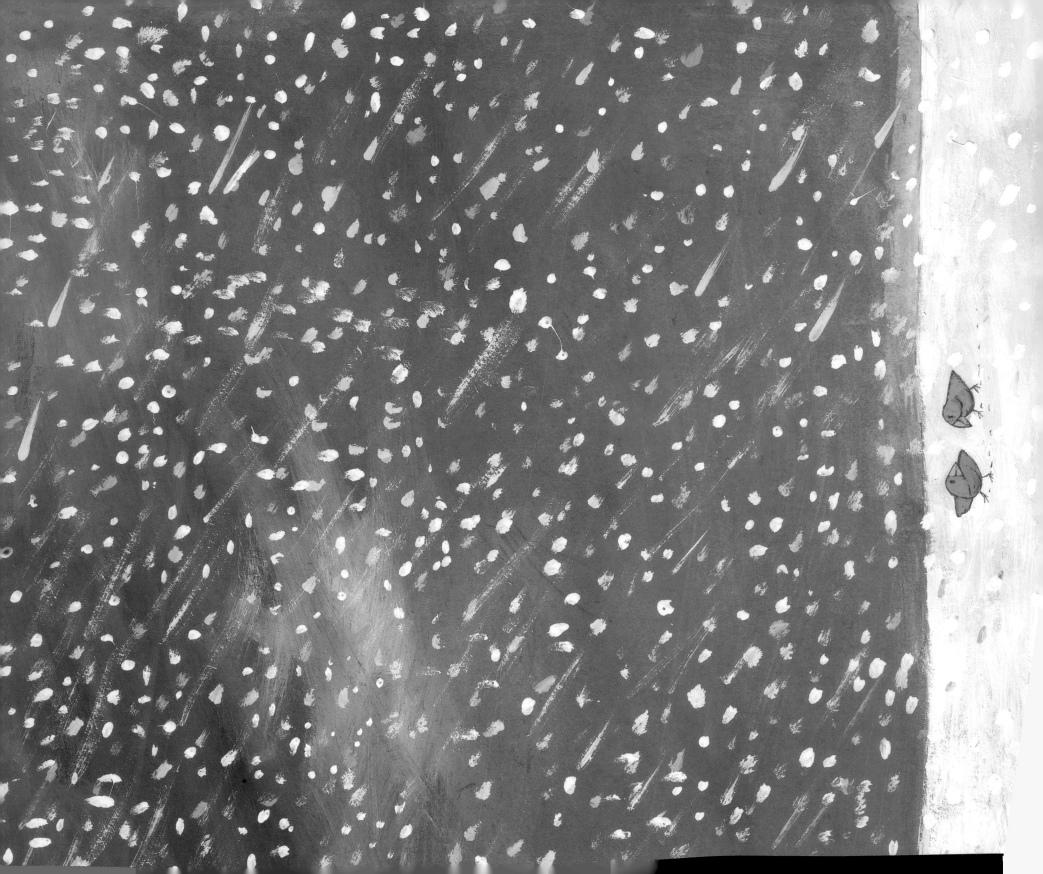

Read more ELMER stories

Also available as a book and CD

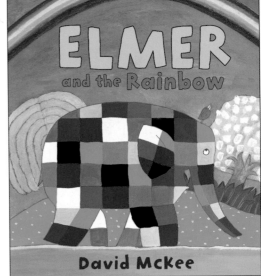

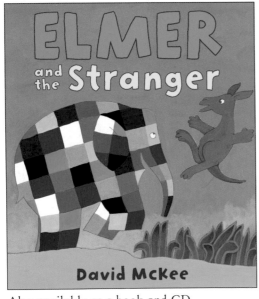
Also available as a book and CD

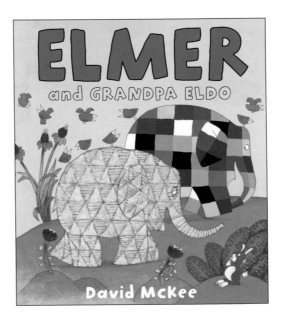

Also available as a book and CD

Find out more about David McKee and Elmer, visit:
www.andersenpress.co.uk/elmer

This ELMER book belongs to:

. . . .